A NORTH - SOUTH PAPERBACK

Critical praise for

Midnight Rider

"A good story for young horse lovers."   *Booklist*

"The poetic pleasure of the young girl's stolen ride . . . is seductive, particularly when coupled with Heyne's starlit watercolors . . . which show an ethereally lovely horse and a stubborn and credible young rider. Young horse-lovers who like a tinge of magic to their equine dreams will appreciate Charlie's nighttime revel."
Bulletin of the Center for Children's Books

"The coastal setting provides a backdrop of blues and grays. The freckled, red-haired heroine and Starbright seem to blend with the sea and shore, and the scenes of them galloping along the sand make the book memorable. The text flows smoothly, and the story may lead readers to similar seaside horse tales."   *School Library Journal*

Krista Ruepp

Midnight Rider

Illustrated by Ulrike Heyne

Translated by J. Alison James

North-South Books

NEW YORK / LONDON

Copyright © 1995 by Nord-Süd Verlag AG, Gossau Zürich, Switzerland.
First published in Switzerland under the title *Mitternachtsreiter*
English translation copyright © 1995 by North-South Books Inc.
All rights reserved. No part of this book may be reproduced or utilized in any form
or by any means, electronic or mechanical, including photocopying,
recording, or any information storage and retrieval system,
without permission in writing from the publisher.

First published in the United States, Great Britain, Canada,
Australia, and New Zealand in 1995 by North-South Books,
an imprint of Nord-Süd Verlag AG, Gossau Zürich, Switzerland.
First paperback edition published in 1996.
Distributed in the United States by North-South Books Inc., New York.

Library of Congress Cataloging-in-Publication Data
Ruepp, Krista.
[Mitternachtsreiter. English]
Midnight rider / Krista Ruepp ; illustrated by Ulrike Heyne ;
translated by J. Alison James.
Summary: Charlie becomes friends with Mr. Grimm through her love for his horse,
and the two of them share a secret that even wise Old Fig doesn't know.
[1. Horses—Fiction. 2. Friendship—Fiction. 3. Secrets—Fiction.]
I. Heyne, Ulrike, Ill. II. James, J. Alison. III. Title.
PZ7.R88535Mi 1995
[E]—dc20 95-12321
A CIP catalogue record for this book is available
from The British Library.

*For more information about our books,
and the authors and artists who create them, visit our web site:*
http://www.northsouth.com

ISBN 1-55858-494-3 (TRADE BINDING)
1 3 5 7 9 TB 10 8 6 4 2
ISBN 1-55858-495-1 (LIBRARY BINDING)
1 3 5 7 9 LB 10 8 6 4 2
ISBN 1-55858-620-2 (PAPERBACK)
3 5 7 9 PB 10 8 6 4 2
Printed in Belgium

The sun had just gone down over
Outhorn.

"Mark my words," Old Fig said to
Charlie. "Tonight is a night when ghosts
will be out." He took a long draw on his
pipe.

Old Fig and the girl stood in the dusk, high up on the dunes, and looked out over the sea.

"What ghosts?" asked Charlie.

"The spirits of drowned sailors floating in the waves." Old Fig loved to tell scary stories.

Charlie shivered. The fog rose up and curled its fingers over the little island.

"Time to go in, child," Old Fig said. "It'll be a bad night out here—why, even the Midnight Rider may be abroad."

Charlie smiled to herself. She knew
something about the Midnight Rider—
something that even wise Old Fig didn't
know. . . .

It had all begun after Charlie's old horse died. She had learned to ride on that horse. He hadn't been a fast horse, but he was wonderful all the same. When he died, her parents bought a tractor. Then their farm had cows, sheep, hens, geese and ducks, and a pig—but no horse. So Charlie, who loved horses more than anything, started visiting Starbright.

Starbright was a magnificent stallion
who belonged to Old Man Grimm.
He kept him in the paddock next to his
run-down house.

Old Man Grimm, whose real name was Matthew Grimm, had lived in the old house for as long as anybody could remember. He was not well liked. He always seemed so cold and sullen. No one spoke to him when he went into the village, and he spoke no more than necessary. As soon as he returned to his old house, people whispered about him.

"With a name like Grimm, and a face to match, he can't have a good bone in his body," said Grandma Asa.

Whenever Charlie went to see
Starbright, she always brought something
for him—a carrot, a piece of bread, or an
apple. As soon as the horse caught sight
of the girl, he trotted over, whinnying.
This was how they became friends.

Charlie's greatest dream was to ride on Starbright's back—just once—over the soft sand on the beach. She knew she'd have to ask Old Man Grimm, but she didn't dare. At least not until she saw him one day in the bakery. She gathered all her courage and said, "Mr. Grimm, could I please ride Starbright just once?"

Mr. Grimm glared at her.

"Leave me alone," Grimm said. "I don't have time for children."

Sadly, Charlie left the shop.

That night, Charlie kept having the same dream: She was riding Starbright at a gallop along the beach. The waves rolled onto the sand and the water sprayed up from the horse's hooves. But then Starbright stopped abruptly. Charlie lost her grip and fell to the sand. "I don't have time for children," Starbright said.

The light from the full moon shone
right in Charlie's face. The wind picked
up, and rattled a tree branch against the
window: *clatta-tap!* Charlie woke up.

Quietly she slipped out of bed, pulled on her clothes, and tiptoed out of the house.

She wasn't afraid of the dark tonight.
As she headed for Grimm's farm, her only
thoughts were of Starbright.

She groped her way cautiously towards
the stable. As she took Starbright's bridle
from the tack room, the bit clinked softly
in her hands, and inside the house a dog
barked.

Charlie ran to the paddock and climbed
over the fence. "Starbright!" she
whispered.

A gust of wind blew a white mist across
the field, making it glow in the bright
light of the moon. For a moment the horse
seemed to vanish. Then the wind flicked
up his mane and Starbright trotted over to
his friend. His soft nose smelled like fresh
grass.

Charlie put on the bridle and opened
the gate. She led Starbright to a tree
stump, climbed up, and, with a swing,
landed on his back.

Finally! Finally her dream was coming true! Charlie's heart pounded with excitement. Starbright shook his head impatiently and snorted. Charlie felt safe on his back. If there was one thing she could do, it was ride a horse.

The sand shone white in the moonlight.
Crowns of foam danced on the swelling
breakers as they crashed on the shore.
The girl urged the horse towards the
water's edge.

The wind was at their back. Storm squalls battled over the sky. Charlie and the horse seemed to be part of the waves, the sand, and the sea, alone on the beach. But they were not alone!

Old Fig was watching from the top of the dunes. This was another night he couldn't sleep. Whenever a storm was coming, he could feel it in his bones. Then he would go to the dunes and look out at the sea. He knew the sea better than anyone on the island. He had warned the islanders so often about coming storms that the people said he had premonitions. Everybody listened to his advice. But tonight what he saw from his place on the dunes was enough to frighten even him: A white horse galloped through the spray with a rider on its back! The horse didn't seem to even touch the ground. Then they disappeared into the surf, only to emerge a minute later.

Black clouds blew in front of the moon, and the darkness swallowed up the ghostly figures. Then Fig was certain: "That there was the very devil himself. I saw him with my own eyes. A bad sign that is, a very bad sign. . . ." Shuddering, he turned to go back home. "The devil himself is out tonight."

The barking dog had woken Grimm.
He went to the window. In the bright
moonlight he could see that the stable
door was open. The paddock gate was
open too. Where could Starbright be? . . .

Matthew Grimm ran out of the house, across the pasture to the top of the dunes, and then down to the beach. The sea was in a turmoil. Whitecaps cracked the waves, and the storm howled in the distance. The man stood thunderstruck when he saw Charlie on Starbright.

"Just wait till I get my hands on you!" cried the man into the wind. He was boiling with rage. But at the same time he couldn't help but admire her. That was one brave little girl! And she rode like the devil. Starbright himself looked magnificent. Blast it anyway! It *was* impressive! Nevertheless, he was still going to give her a piece of his mind.

Charlie and Starbright reached the southern point of the beach and turned back. The storm was getting stronger by the minute. Now the stallion was racing against the wind. His nostrils flared.

Suddenly a burst of strength ripped through Starbright. He raced across the sand as if he had wings. Violent, whipping wings.

Charlie tugged on the reins with all her might, but she could no longer hold the horse.

She dug her fingers into his whipping
mane. For the first time she was afraid.

Starbright made a flying leap over a piece of driftwood. Charlie lost her grip and was flung in a high arc. She landed on the sand, and lay there unconscious. The stallion never paused, but galloped up into the dunes, right past Mr. Grimm.

Grimm scanned the shoreline. There lay the girl, at the edge of the sea.

A gigantic wave was welling close to shore. If it broke over Charlie, she would be swept deep under the cold water. Grimm ran. With seconds to spare, he pulled her to safety.

Matthew Grimm carried Charlie back to his house. Just as he was covering her with a blanket, she opened her eyes.

"Where . . . where am I?" Charlie asked.

"Don't be afraid," said the man gently. "I brought you back to my house."

After a while Mr. Grimm said, "Starbright is in the paddock again. You had amazing luck. You could have been killed when Starbright threw you! Now you see why you should never ride a horse you don't know."

Charlie sniffed. "But I *do* know
Starbright. . . ." she said.

"Here, let me make us some tea," said
Mr. Grimm. "Then we can talk."

Grimm handed Charlie a warm cup.
Then he spoke. "When that horse feels

the wind in his face, he gets charged with energy. You couldn't have known that, but he can be very dangerous."

Charlie sipped her tea. Finally she spoke. "Will I ever be allowed to ride Starbright again?"

"Hmmm." Mr. Grimm thought for a moment. "All right, but never alone!"

When Charlie had finished her tea, Mr.
Grimm took her back home. Quietly she
slipped into her room and crawled into
bed. Her parents hadn't even noticed that
she had been gone. "Mr. Grimm isn't so
bad after all," she thought as she drifted
off to sleep.

"Hey, lazybones! Rustle your feathers!" Her mother had to wake her the next morning.

Dazed, she sat at the breakfast table, forgetting to eat.

"You look tired," her father said. "Didn't you sleep well?"

"Oh . . . I hardly slept at all. Last night I went for a ride on Starbright, down at the beach, and—" but her father interrupted: "That was just another one of your dreams. It seemed real because of the storm. Now off to school, or you'll be late."

That morning Old Fig struggled through the roar of the storm. "I knew it. I just knew it," he murmured. He was on his way to warn the islanders whose animals were still out in the pastures. "The sea will flood the fields for sure," he cried to the people. "Bring in the animals!"

But he didn't say anything about the ghostly Midnight Rider. He didn't want to worry them more than necessary when they had a storm coming.

By afternoon the storm had let up a bit. When Charlie went down to Mr. Grimm's, Starbright was already in his stall, and Mr. Grimm had given him fresh hay. "Good thing you came," he said. "I could use some help."

Together they took care of the horse.

"It's nice that you came to visit us," Mr. Grimm said shyly.

"Us?" asked Charlie.

"Yes. Sometimes we're very alone out here, Starbright, the dog, and I," said the man. He lit a fire in the wood stove and made some cocoa.

"Charlie, tell me honestly." Mr. Grimm cleared his throat. "Why won't the people in the village have anything to do with me? They say, 'Here comes the Grimm,' and when my back is turned, they put their heads together and—"

"Because you always have such a nasty expression on your face," Charlie explained.

"Really? You think so?" Mr. Grimm's
face broke into a rare grin. "Well, perhaps
you're right." He looked thoughtfully into
the fire for a long time after that, as they
sat silently sipping their cocoa.

After the storm there were long gloomy
days of rain.

From three directions, three figures,
wrapped and bundled, trudged through the
puddles and met in the bakery: Old Fig,
Mr. Grimm, and Charlie.

"My oh my, and a good afternoon to you all!" Mr. Grimm greeted all the people in the shop.

Shocked, they returned his greeting.

"Charlie," said Old Fig. "Did you hear about the Midnight Rider?" And then he told her the story about the ghostly rider who came out of the night to warn about the hurricane. "He galloped on a pure white horse through the sea, and in the morning the fields were all under water." Old Fig lowered his voice to a whisper. "He rode like the wind of the storm. Only the devil himself can ride like that! You have to believe me. . . ."

The people in the shop held their breath. But Mr. Grimm and Charlie winked at each other and had to bite back their laughter.

Grandma Asa had listened spellbound to the story. "I'll have to tell the ladies," she muttered, and she soon made sure that the story of the Midnight Rider was known by all on the island.

From then on, the people often went
to the cliffs and looked for signs of the
Midnight Rider.

The days went by, and as often as
Charlie had time, she visited Mr. Grimm.
She fed and brushed Starbright,

and when she rode the stallion on the beach, Mr. Grimm would run alongside with his dog.

Sometimes they met Old Fig on the beach, and he walked with them for a while. Fig liked that Grimm always listened to his ghost stories.

Charlie and the stallion Starbright became a common sight on that island. But no one, not even Old Fig, who had the power to predict storms, realized that Charlie was the mysterious Midnight Rider. The secret of that stormy night belonged only to Charlie, Mr. Grimm, and Starbright.

Krista Ruepp was born in Cologne,
Germany. After studying to be a teacher, she
worked as an editor for a German television
network, then in advertising and marketing.
For young readers, she has written stories,
poetry, and songs. She now lives in
Remschied, Germany, with her husband
and their two sons.

Ulrike Heyne was born in Dresden, Germany. She studied fashion illustration and graphic design in Munich, and then spent several years working in advertising and teaching painting and drawing.
She lives with her husband in Sachsen, Germany, not far from the city where she was born.

North-South Easy-to-Read Books

Rinaldo, the Sly Fox
by Ursel Scheffler, illustrated by Iskender Gider

The Return of Rinaldo, the Sly Fox
by Ursel Scheffler, illustrated by Iskender Gider

Rinaldo on the Run
by Ursel Scheffler, illustrated by Iskender Gider

Loretta and the Little Fairy
by Gerda Marie Scheidl,
illustrated by Christa Unzner-Fischer

Little Polar Bear and the Brave Little Hare
by Hans de Beer

Where's Molly?
by Uli Waas

**The Extraordinary Adventures
of an Ordinary Hat**
by Wolfram Hänel,
illustrated by Christa Unzner-Fischer

Mia the Beach Cat
by Wolfram Hänel, illustrated by Kirsten Höcker

The Old Man and the Bear
by Wolfram Hänel,
illustrated by Jean-Pierre Corderoc'h

Lila's Little Dinosaur
by Wolfram Hänel, illustrated by Alex de Wolf

Meet the Molesons
by Burny Bos, illustrated by Hans de Beer

More from the Molesons
by Burny Bos, illustrated by Hans de Beer

On the Road with Poppa Whopper
by Marianne Busser and Ron Schröder,
illustrated by Hans de Beer

Spiny
by Jürgen Lassig,
illustrated by Uli Waas